W9-BFF-036

WINDMILL

Michael Bond

pictures by Tony Cattaneo

Studio Vista

Copyright © Michael Bond 1975
Pictures copyright © Tony Cattaneo 1975
All rights reserved. No part of this publication
may be reproduced, stored in a retrieval system, or
transmitted, in any form or by any means, without
the prior permission of Studio Vista.
First published in Great Britain 1975
Printed in Great Britain by Hazell Watson & Viney Ltd,
Aylesbury, Bucks

ISBN 0 289 70452 9

Windmill is a donkey.
He is short and stubby, and he lives on the island of Crete.

But his fame has spread far and wide.
People who know about these things nudge each other when
they see him coming, and they always treat him with great respect,
for they still remember the day he first came by his name, high
up in the mountains on the Plain of a Thousand Windmills.

In those days he was known simply as 'Old Hee-Haw'.

The plain where he lived was green and fertile, and it was kept that way by water drawn up out of the earth by all the windmills.

There used to be almost as many donkeys as there were windmills, and Hee-Haw and his friends spent their time carrying the produce from the plain to the towns and villages at the foot of the mountain.

Hee-Haw was reckoned to be the strongest of all the donkeys, and he was happy in his work, asking for nothing except food and water and somewhere to rest at night.

"Hee-Haw! Hee-Haw!" he used to go as he scrambled down the rocky slopes.
"Watch me! Watch me!
"See how much I can carry!"

And then one morning he heard a strange noise.
"Honk! Honk!
"Beep! Beep! Beep!" The noise grew louder and louder every moment.

Suddenly he had to jump for his life as a huge lorry piled high with fruit and vegetables roared into view.
"Honk! Honk!" it went gleefully as it thundered past.
"Beep! Beep! Beep!
"Watch me! Watch me!
"I'll be in the market before you!"

Hee-Haw could hardly believe his eyes.

But there was worse to come.
The very next day he met two lorries, and the day after that there were three.
Soon there were lorries everywhere, and the once peaceful mountainside began to echo to the sound of their horns.

"Honk! Honk!" they went, as they swept past in a cloud of dust.
"Beep! Beep! Beep!"

"Mind out, old Hee-Haw," they seemed to be saying.
"Out of our way.
"We have work to do.
"Honk! Honk!
"Beep! Beep! Beep!
"We can carry more than you.
"Ten times as much in half the time.
"We can't think why you bother.
"It's time you were put out to graze."

And it was true.
No matter how hard the donkeys worked they barely had time
to reach the bottom of the mountain before the lorries were
on their way back up again, ready for the next load.

The farmers grew rich, and being rich wanted to become richer
still. Land which had grown only one crop was now made to
grow a second, and one by one the donkeys began to disappear.

Most of them accepted their fate, for it was the way of the
world. But Hee-Haw refused to give in. Bowed under the
weight of his load, his leathery lungs swollen to twice their
normal size, he struggled after the lorries.
"Hee-Haw!" he cried.
"Hee-Haw! Hee-Haw!
"Just you wait!
"I'll show you!"

But the more he struggled the more the lorries honked at him,
and the faster they went. It seemed as though nothing could stop
them.

And then suddenly there was a change in the weather.
The wind dropped and all the windmills stopped turning.
Such a thing had never been known before and gradually
an enormous quiet settled over the plain.

The faces of the villagers grew longer and longer as time
went by and they saw their crops start to wither and die under
the hot sun.

"What shall we do?" they cried in despair.
"Without wind our sails won't turn.
"And if the sails won't turn the pumps won't work.
"And if the pumps don't work we shall have no water.
"And without water we shall have no crops.
"And without crops we shall starve."

"Perhaps it's the calm before the storm," said some.
"Perhaps when the wind blows again it will blow twice as hard."

But the elders of the village shook their heads.
"It is a punishment," they said. "It is a punishment for
being so greedy. It will need a miracle to put things right.
And miracles only happen to those who deserve them."

Hee-Haw felt sad as he gazed round at the empty plain.
"If only *I* could do something to help." he thought.

He gave a deep sigh, and as he did so the dried-up grass at his feet rippled in the still air and an idea floated up into his mind.

Hee-Haw grew more and more excited as he thought the matter over. He *did* have one thing that no-one else had, and that was the biggest pair of lungs on the island. Lungs that had grown larger and tougher still through chasing after all the lorries.

Gathering himself together, he stood up and took a deep breath, filling them so full of air it felt as if they would burst. Then he looked around for the nearest windmill.

At first, no matter how hard he blew, nothing happened.
But he puffed and he puffed, and all at once there was a creak from
the sail as the canvas billowed out and it started to turn. The breeze
from the first windmill blew against a second, and a moment later
that, too, began to turn. Soon there was an answering creak from a
third windmill. Then a fourth and a fifth.

The sound brought the villagers rushing from their homes.
"The wind!" they cried. "The wind has come at last!"
And then they paused, hardly able to believe their eyes, as
they saw what was happening.

Suddenly one of them sounded the horn on his lorry.
"Honk! Honk!
"Beep! Beep! Beep!"
"Come on!" he shouted.
"Come on, Hee-Haw!
"Blow! Blow!
"Blow as hard as you can!"

"Honk! Honk!
"Beep! Beep! Beep!" One after another the other horns in
the village joined in.
The noise was deafening.

It woke the other donkeys, and when they saw what was happening
they followed Hee-Haw's lead and began to run hither and thither,
in and out of the windmills, blowing for all they were worth. The
steam from their nostrils rose and formed a tiny cloud, and the
draught from the sails carried it up into the sky until it reached a point
where it seemed to hover for a moment and then turn in on itself,
swirling and whirling as it formed a new and stronger wind, sucking
air from all around.

Soon all the windmills were turning; faster than they had ever
turned before, and the fresh, cold water came gushing up out
of the earth to flood the plain.

There was dancing and feasting all that night on the Plain of a Thousand Windmills. People from miles around came to congratulate Hee-Haw and all the other donkeys and to give thanks. And so that his deed would never be forgotten they decided that from that moment on they would always call him WINDMILL.

Windmill no longer minds when he sees the lorries on his mountain, for he knows that not all of them put together could ever have done what he did.

They seem to know it too, for they always pull in to the side of the road when they see him coming, and sometimes the drivers lean out of the cab in order to give him a carrot or two.
And as he goes on his way they give him a friendly toot.
"Honk! Honk!
"Beep! Beep! Beep!"
"Good old Windmill!" they seem to be saying.
"Where would we be without you ?"